whenever there is danger send for...

Kung-Fu
Pigs

Scholastic Children's Books,
Commonwealth House, 1–19 New Oxford Street,
London, WC1A 1NU, UK
A division of Scholastic Ltd
London ~ New York ~ Toronto ~ Sydney ~ Auckland
Mexico City ~ New Delhi ~ Hong Kong

First published in the UK by Scholastic Ltd, 2004

Copyright © Keith Brumpton, 2004

ISBN 0 439 96857 7

All rights reserved

Printed and bound by AIT Nørhaven A/S, Denmark

10 9 8 7 6 5 4 3 2 1

Kung-Fu Pigs

Curse of the Vampire Squirrels

Keith Brumpton

■SCHOLASTIC

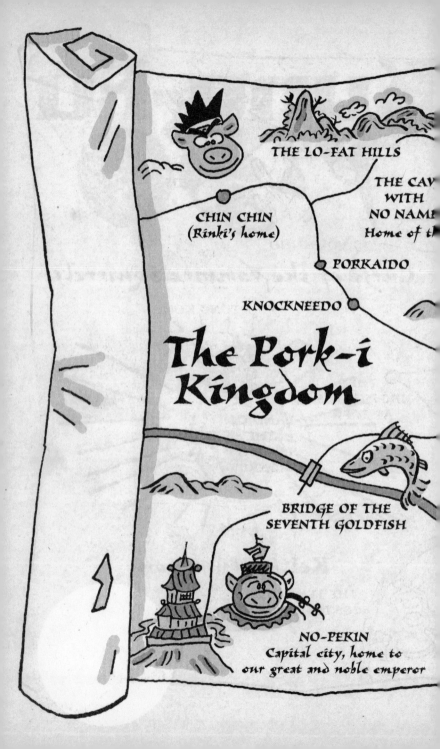

THE LO-FAT HILLS

THE CAV
WITH
NO NAME
Home of t

CHIN CHIN
(Rinki's home)

PORKAIDO

KNOCKNEEDO

The Pork-i Kingdom

BRIDGE OF THE
SEVENTH GOLDFISH

NO-PEKIN
Capital city, home to
our great and noble emperor

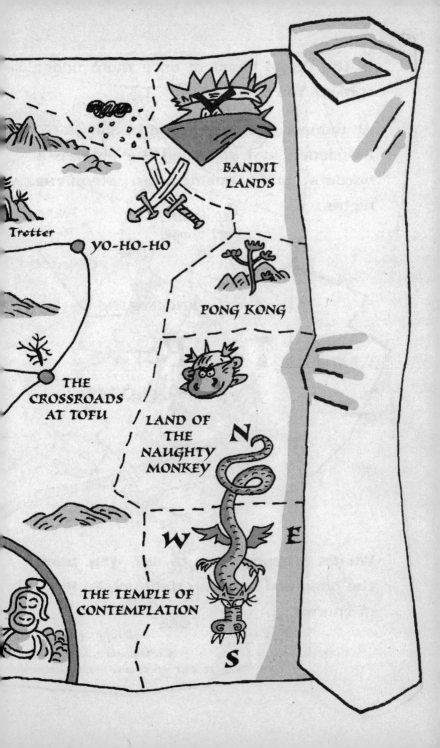

Is the Pork-i kingdom once more under threat? You bet!

All manner of wolves, bandits and up-to-no-gooders are attacking the emperor's borders and causing him sleepless nights.

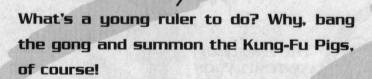

What's a young ruler to do? Why, bang the gong and summon the Kung-Fu Pigs, of course!

Curse of the Vampire Squirrels

Translated from the original Pork-i manuscript by Keith Brumpton

PROLOGUE

From my long white beard and wrinkled trotters you will know me as Oinky No Ho, venerable Priest of Wu-Dah-Ling and adviser to the emperor.

Come, sit upon this shady seat and I will tell you of the time when the Kung-Fu Pigs were summoned to our great city of No-Pekin, and given a mission which many thought impossible. It is a tale of daring, danger, and squirrels with very sharp fangs. There are moments that will draw you to the edge of your chair and quicken the beating of your heart.

Battles that will delight the old soldier and young warrior alike. And there is romance too, with a pig princess whose legendary beauty leaves even poets short of words.

But enough of this! If you are ready, honourable stranger, I will begin...

CHAPTER 1

"Pigs in glass palaces shouldn't throw wobblers."

Wo-No, court poet, X Dynasty

Emperor Ping-Pong was in a bad mood that morning. He was seated in the throne room of the Green Dragon, ready for his weekly meeting with Oinky No Ho, his chief adviser.

'You'

This was when the emperor learnt news of his kingdom. And today, as usual, it was bad news: the crops had failed …

his armies had been defeated …

and worst of all … the new silk slippers he had ordered still hadn't arrived.

Whilst Oinky No Ho gave his report, the emperor sat and listened impatiently.

His nanny, Manki Hanki, was in the throne room too, arranging the young emperor's hair. She pulled his pigtails back so tight it brought tears to his eyes.

"This is terrible," he squeaked.

"I know, your Tinyness." Oinky No Ho bowed. "Never have we lost so many battles in one week."

"No, no," spluttered the young emperor. "I mean about my hair. Can't I wear it in a fringe?"

"Big emperors don't cry," answered Manki Hanki, briskly, and continued brushing and tugging.

Ouch!

Oinky No Ho took a deep breath and tried once more to gain the emperor's attention.

"Our kingdom is under attack from all sides, your Nobleness. Our armies keep running away. I think it is time to make peace with our neighbours."

"I'd rather bash them up!" Ping-Pong giggled.

"Unfortunately our enemies are much bigger and stronger than us."

The emperor sucked his thumb, angrily. Oinky No Ho seized his chance. "What I propose, your  Nothingness, is a marriage alliance."

"A wedding," cried Ping-Pong, clapping his trotters together excitedly. "I love a good wedding. Who's getting married?"

You.

Me?!

"Yes, your Haughtiness, I propose that you should marry a princess of the Bling Dynasty."

The young emperor suddenly looked worried and pale. "I… I'm not sure. Won't I have to share all my treasure with her?"

"Oh no," answered the wise Oinky No Ho. "It is quite the reverse. I have arranged that you will receive twenty thousand golden dumplings as part of your bride's wedding dowry."

In an instant the colour had returned to the emperor's cheeks. "Oh goody! Golden dumplings ... my favourite!"

Then another thought came into his mind. (Two in one day, this was quite unusual.)

"...What if I don't like the look of this princess?"

Oinky No Ho smiled calmly. "I have thought of that too."

From beneath his gown he produced a small painting, covered with a silk cloth.

"This is a recent portrait of the lady in question."

"...her name is Princess Yukkifoto..."
The emperor's eyes suddenly glazed over.

She's nothing special. Her eyes are too close together.

But Manki Hanki wasn't so impressed.

"With your permission," continued Oinky No Ho, "I will send for the Kung-Fu Pigs and they will escort your Porkiness to the kingdom of Pong Kong, where the princess and her people live."

Ping-Pong reluctantly tore himself away from the picture of the princess.

The Kung-Fu Pigs? But I thought we only summoned them in times of great danger?

Oinky No Ho gave a little cough and exited the room without looking back.

"The danger is greater than your Majesty could possibly know," he muttered to himself as he made his way across the courtyard.

Moments later came the sound of the great gong being struck...

CHAPTER 2

*"Fortune favours the brave.
And very fast runners."*
General Chin-Tuk, 2nd century

Noble Rinki was grooming his pony, Desert Wind, when the sound of the great gong reached his ears.

He grabbed hold of the reins and leapt into the saddle, for he knew that the gong was his summons to the emperor's aid.

Meanwhile, many miles hence, that fine figure of a samurai fighting pig, Stinki, had just finished chopping a huge pile of vegetables ...

This will be a dish to remember!

... when the gong sounded.

DONG!

I don't believe it! It's that gong again. I'll have to leave this to stew!

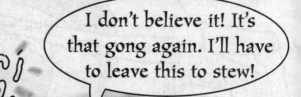

In the peaceful Temple of the Blue Stream, where it was so peaceful the sound of a leaf falling was like a thunder of hooves, the gentle and wise Dinki was deep in contemplation ...

Er ... ommmm

... as the sound of the great gong reached her.

DONG!

I must leave these peaceful thoughts behind – for, in times of danger, it is our first duty to help the emperor.

Soon the three Kung-Fu Pigs were hurrying across the kingdom, towards the great city of No-Pekin, where the emperor was preparing to make a journey far more dangerous than he knew!

CHAPTER 3

"At the bottom of a hole there's usually something dark."
Old Pekinese song

As the Kung-Fu Pigs were busy answering their emperor's call, elsewhere in Ping-Pong's kingdom, his greatest enemy was equally busy laying evil plans. The Crimson Trotter was the name of that most untrustworthy of pigs, and fearful was his name to all who walk the path of peace.

The Crimson Trotter's secret lair lay in a cave reached only by means of several long and smelly tunnels.

Lit by the light of a flaming torch, he paced up and down, awaiting the arrival of his messenger. At last he heard footsteps, and a shadowy figure emerged into the dim light. He greeted the messenger with a gruff nod of his crimson-capped head.

"Emperor Ping-Pong is setting out on a great journey," hissed the messenger, a wolf with breathing difficulties. "He travels to the Hi-lands. There he is to be married to the Princess Yukkifoto."

The Crimson Trotter's eyes took on an even more evil gleam. He rubbed his trotters together and clicked his teeth. "Excellent! Excellent!"

"You're pleased then?" answered the wolf messenger.

The Crimson Trotter began to stalk the cave like an evil genius, which of course is exactly what he was.

"Oh, I'm pleased all right. The Hi-lands are perfect territory for an ambush."

Ambush?

"Yes … a surprise attack that will remove that pipsqueak of an emperor at a stroke, opening the way for me to seize the throne that is wrongly mine! Once in power, I can get rid of that white-bearded do-gooder, Oinky No Ho, and all the treasures of the kingdom will be in my possession."

"I'm with you so far," the wolf wheezed.

"I want you to go and prepare a secret ambush. Wait while I write out your orders. This is going to be my greatest plan ever!"

Not hard, considering all the other ones failed.

The Crimson Trotter let out a great laugh, which echoed out across the cave and down the winding tunnels until it vanished into the dark and desolate forest that surrounded his hideout…

Haha hahahahahaha

CHAPTER 4

*"The end of one journey
is the start of the next."*
Confuse-us, 3rd century philoso-pig

Back at the emperor's palace, Oinky No Ho greeted the Kung-Fu Pigs as they arrived, weary from their journey.

Welcome, noble warriors.

"Shake the dust from your clogs but be prepared for more miles upon the road," said Oinky No Ho as he led them indoors. Waiting inside the great hall was a table laden with refreshments.

"Are we going on a trip?" asked Stinki, eating hungrily from a bowl of rice.

Oinky No Ho nodded slowly. "The emperor is to be married."

Oinky No Ho began to unroll a large parchment. "She is a princess of the Bling Dynasty. And the wedding is to be held in her homeland."

"That is very far from here," murmured Dinki, with a look of concern.

"Yes," nodded their noble and ancient guru. "The journey will be long and dangerous, for it will take you and the emperor into the Hi-lands of Hoki-Koki."

Stinki almost choked on his rice. "But that's where the Vampire Squirrels live ... if you call that living."

"Vampire Squirrels?" interrupted Rinki, who seemed to be the only one who hadn't heard of them. Oinky No Ho sat down in his chair and took a deep breath...

Let me explain...

"The Vampire Squirrels once lived amongst ordinary folk like you and I … and they weren't even vampires in those days…

"But then in the No-Kashi period, widespread famine came to the land and the squirrels grew desperate. Chronicles tell how they were reduced to feeding upon their own kind in order to stay alive.

Anyone got any noodles?

"The Emperor Yora-Kuti banished them from the Pork-i kingdom and so began a great wandering in the wilderness, until, led by their leader, Sho-Me-A-Wei-In, they came to the Hi-lands of Hoki-Koki, where they eventually settled.

"Gradually the Vampire Squirrels developed into great warriors. They were bloodthirsty foes, who fought only at night.

"Theirs is a land of snow and mist, which only the very brave or the very foolish would think of entering.

"Their main weapons are their sharp teeth ...

... their incredible agility ...

... and a long fighting stick called a Naginata.

"Defeating the Vampire Squirrels is not easy. It is best to fight them during daylight. They do not like fire, or prayers chanted by a woman's voice…

"Anyone bitten by them will become one of the great undead, pale in complexion and muddled in thought.

"This is the curse of the Vampire Squirrels, and that is all you need to know for now…"

"I hope we can keep our emperor safe from them," said Dinki, when Oinky No Ho had finished his tale.

"We will!" thundered Stinki. "You know you can rely on us."

Oinky No Ho closed his eyes and stroked his beard, thoughtfully. "The task ahead will not be an easy one, my friends. Dark forces are stirring. You must be sure the emperor eats plenty of garlic and does not venture out after dark."

"Got any pictures of the princess?" asked Rinki, who was by nature a very curious young pig.

CHAPTER 5

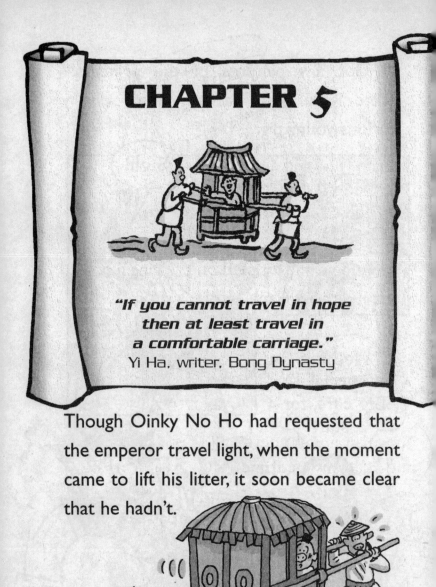

**"If you cannot travel in hope
then at least travel in
a comfortable carriage."**
Yi Ha, writer, Bong Dynasty

Though Oinky No Ho had requested that the emperor travel light, when the moment came to lift his litter, it soon became clear that he hadn't.

And he had insisted on bringing along his nanny, Manki Hanki, too.

As Rinki watched how slowly the emperor's litter moved, with all his possessions travelling behind, he gave a worried sigh.

"If we continue at this pace we will be vulnerable to attack."

Stinki finished off a couple of chop-suey rolls. "So what? We can handle it."

Dinki was gazing off into the distance. "Yes, but this time we have the emperor to protect!" she said.

...Finally, they reached the foothills of the Hi-Lands, where the difficult part of the trip would really begin.

Heavy rain had made the mountain pass dangerous. One slip could send a careless pig tumbling to his or her doom, while the weight of the emperor's possessions slowed their progress to a snail's pace...

The Kung-Fu Pigs tried to quicken the pace.

Eventually, after much huffing and puffing, the emperor's wedding convoy reached a narrow and rickety rope bridge, known as the Pass of the Thousand Foot Drop. Why it was known as that, no one knew.

Rinki's brow furrowed. "I'm sure he'll see reason."

Dinki tried patiently to explain. "But your Royalness, the bridge could break at any time. If we don't lighten the load, we're putting everyone at risk."

"Fooey," replied the emperor, who usually won arguments.

Manki Hanki joined in the discussion. "There's not a single thing among the emperor's possessions that he can do without."

"Yeah," added Ping-Pong. "Now take me across that bridge!"

The three Kung-Fu Pigs saw that they must obey their emperor's orders. They decided they would each cross the bridge in turn, beginning with the emperor and his possessions, because they were the heaviest and the bridge would be at its strongest for the first crossing.

The weight of Ping-Pong, his courtiers, and all his gold and finery was almost too much for the rickety rope bridge, which creaked and groaned in the most terrifying manner. But the emperor made it across safely.

A lot of fuss about nothing.

They too were safe!

Rinki followed, taking a great leap and landing on the muddy bank.

Only Stinki now remained. He was the largest of the Kung-Fu Pigs and Dinki was worried.

Be careful!

Don't worry! I'm light on my trotters you know...

Within the blink of an eye, Stinki had vanished into the raging river below. Rinki hid his eyes, unable to look.

We always knew it would be dangerous, but I never imagined this. Poor Stinki...

Dinki called out, "Stinki! Stinki!" but there was no reply, only the sound of the waters raging beneath them and of Dinki's voice, echoing forlornly down the valley...

Later, Dinki lit a candle for her friend and Rinki listened to her prayers with a tear in his eye.

> Enjoy the great pigsty in the sky, dear friend.

The emperor blew his snout into a fine silk handkerchief.

"Now I've only got two guards instead of three," he grumbled. "What a terrible day."

CHAPTER 6

"The wise pig will always listen for danger before meeting it."
So-Fa-Gon, writer, 2nd century

"So this is the land of the Vampire Squirrels?" whispered Rinki as they approached a dark pine forest, coiled in mist. "…At least, that's what the sign says."

Tall trees began to block out the light and darkness was falling.

"Are we there yet?" squeaked Ping-Pong, from his litter.

"Not quite, your Highness," answered Rinki. "But we must camp here for the night."

"Camp?" asked the emperor. "What's that?"

Luckily Manki Hanki was on hand to explain, and once she had offered to tell the young ruler a bedtime story all objections were ended.

But then it's candles out at nine.

Rinki and Dinki decided to keep watch together since neither felt sleepy.

"So one bite from one of these squirrels would turn us into zombies?" asked Rinki with a look of concern.

That is what the local legends say. Let us hope we never find out.

And so the night grew darker, and the only sound was the high-pitched snore coming from the emperor's litter. Or at least it was until Dinki heard something out in the woods...

It was midnight and the Vampire Squirrels had begun their attack! From out of the gloomy woods floated squirrels with sharp fangs, blood-red eyes, and their famous fighting sticks, the Naginata.

The two remaining Kung-Fu Pigs drew their own weapons in readiness…

There were squirrels to the left of them and squirrels to the right of them. Into the valley of squirrels advanced the Kung-Fu Pigs.

Rinki and Dinki battled the vampires using the tactics Oinky No Ho had shown them. Rinki held aloft a flaming torch, knowing how they hated fire...

...Whilst Dinki used a combination of her fighting staff and some ancient Shin-toe prayers.

The Vampire Squirrels were skilled with their Naginata and nimble on their feet.

The Kung-Fu Pigs had to use all their fighting skills just to stay in one piece.

The noise of the battle reached Ping-Pong's carriage.

Woken from his beauty sleep, he sent his nanny, Manki Hanki, to investigate. Then promptly fell back to sleep.

Tch tch, what's all this racket? The emperor won't stand for this, you know. He needs his beauty sleep.

She approached a Vampire Squirrel, dressed from head to foot in a swirling black cloak.

"If you must have a fight to the death, please keep the noise down!" Manki Hanki told the squirrel.

As Oinky No Ho had warned, when bitten by a Vampire Squirrel the victim begins to transform almost at once, and so it was with Ping-Pong's nanny.

I must go back to the emperor...

Out in the woods the battle continued to rage, and Rinki and Dinki found themselves driven back into the woods by the vampire army.

"Didn't think I'd miss out on a good scrap like this, did you?" said Stinki.

Dinki wanted to know how Stinki had saved himself from the raging river.

With Stinki at their side, the tide turned and the Kung-Fu Pigs drove back the Vampire Squirrels until the first glimmer of dawn hit the forest.

The last of the Vampire Squirrels melted away into whatever dark places they inhabited, and the Kung-Fu Pigs were left to catch up on events.

Now you can hear
what happened to me
on that bridge...

"I fell, as you saw, down and down.
For as the proverb
goes, 'A falling pig
travels fast'.

"I was only
saved because
my sword belt
caught on an
overhanging
branch.
TWANG!

"For what seemed an age, I hung there, balanced between life and death. If I'd eaten one more bowl of rice for breakfast I think that branch would have snapped.

"But the branch held, and eventually I managed to struggle my way back along it and then up the cliff. But by then of course you'd gone. I read the prayers you'd written for me. Very touching."

"We're glad to have you back." Rinki smiled.

Yes, welcome back, noble samurai!

The emperor's head appeared out of his litter. "Has anyone seen my nanny? It's time for my breakfast!"

Coming, your Highness!

CHAPTER 7

"Lu took the high road and Li took the low road but Li'll be in Porkland before Lu."
Traditional song, Bling Dynasty

The journey to the Hi-lands took them up, up, and away, beyond the forests and woods and into the mountains. There, the clouds hung low and the rain fell all day.

The young emperor grew more and more bad-tempered, and his nanny, Manki Hanki, seemed to grow paler and paler, and stranger and stranger.

Where is my face cloth, nanny?

I will bring it to you after dark.

"Why do you keep hiding all day, nanny?" quizzed the baffled young emperor.

Now, as it happened, the Kung-Fu Pigs and their party were not the only ones on the winding road that wet and windy autumn day. No ... the spies of the Crimson Trotter were there too, hidden just out of sight...

... and watching in silence.

So it was that the two wolves remained undetected and later, were able to report back to their master with news of the expedition's progress.

The emperor is still heading towards Pong Kong.

The Crimson Trotter's cruel eyes narrowed in a smile. "Those Vampire Squirrels almost ruined my plans, but now the wedding can take place and my little surprise will be the icing on the cake!"

The Crimson Trotter gestured the wolves forward. "And you two had better be dressed for the occasion."

Fourteen days and nights passed before the wedding party finally reached the fortress of Taki-Bashi, where the marriage of His Royal Highness Ping-Pong, and Yukkifoto, princess of the Bling Dynasty, was to take place.

Yukkifoto's father, I-Shu-Koko, was there to greet them.

"Welcome, welcome, noble Ping-Pong..."

Rinki blushed. "Er, I'm not the emperor
… this is his Highness…"

Can I see my
room, please?

Ping-Pong was at once shown to the
most luxurious of rooms, filled with fine
foods, billowing silks, and a large comfy bed.

The Kung-Fu Pigs were camped outside in the rain.

You'd think we might have got to sleep indoors.

It does not matter. At least here we can watch all the comings and goings.

Manki Hanki wandered past, carrying the emperor's toilet bag.

"There's something here that's not quite right but I can't put my trotter on it," Dinki said.

Inside his new room, the emperor was full of excitement. "I can't wait until tomorrow to see my bride. I think I'll send for her now."

The emperor hurried to seek out the bride's father to ask his permission for a meeting. But when he quizzed I-Shu-Koko about seeing the princess that night he was to be disappointed with the reply.

"I'm sorry, but my little princess tells me she is very tired. I am not surprised, she has spent the whole day putting on her make-up."

Ping-Pong returned to his room feeling rather deflated, and ordered his nanny to run him a nice hot bath.

With lots of bubbles.

But Manki Hanki wasn't there to run any hot baths. She was out in the dark and rain, prowling the fortress battlements. Her teeth were long and shiny and her eyes burned red as hot coals.

Ping-Pong spent the evening alone and even had to blow out his own candles.

You just can't get the staff these days.

What will the emperor think on finally seeing his new bride? Has Manki Hanki lost the plot?

Can the Kung-Fu Pigs ensure the big day passes off safely? To find the answers, dear reader, you must hurry to the next chapter.

CHAPTER 8

"Better alive than wed."
Old saying, Bling Dynasty

Magnificent were the decorations in the temple that joyous wedding day, and glad were the hearts of those assembled there.

Ping-Pong was down by the altar, dressed in his finest royal robe, waiting for his new bride to join him. He had over five hundred robes in his collection, it had taken him a long time to choose it.

The temple was silent for a moment, then the court musicians began to play a tune. This was the signal for the bride to walk up the aisle.

At the front of the temple the Kung-Fu Pigs were keeping their eyes open for trouble.

Through the throng of assembled guests they could just glimpse the blushing bride.

She's very tall.

Hard to see much under that veil.

Don't they look nice together?

Watching alongside them was the proud father, I-Shu-Koko, and the rest of the princess's family.

At the entrance to the temple there were also a number of tall figures dressed in dark, hooded robes. I-Shu-Koko didn't recognize them and guessed they must be part of the emperor's party. The Kung-Fu Pigs thought they must be part of the bride's party.

The Princess Yukkifoto arrived next to her husband-to-be, clutching a bouquet of limp dandelions, and together they waited for the priest to begin the service.

Ping-Pong looked up at his bride and noticed that she didn't look much like her portrait.

"My, what big hands you have," he muttered.

"All the better for counting your treasure," she replied.

"And what a long snout you have."

"All the better for sniffing out trouble," the princess replied in a deep voice.

"And my, what sharp teeth you have," observed the young emperor with a gulp.

At which point a crimson-clad figure shouted out from the back of the temple: "Now! Quick! Grab him!"

Princess Yukkifoto suddenly threw off her veil and grabbed the emperor in her large furry paws.

She wasn't a pig princess at all, "she" was a fearsome wolf in the pay of the Crimson Trotter! His dastardly plan looked like it was about to succeed.

Quick! The emperor needs our help!

The Kung-Fu Pigs rushed to the front of the temple where the poor priest was in a state of shock.

"Save the emperor!" shouted Dinki in alarm.

Too late! They've got him!

The emperor was just about to be bundled out of the back of the temple when suddenly Manki Hanki made a timely appearance.

"Nanny!" gasped Ping-Pong, and passed out.

Manki Hanki's looks had certainly changed since she'd been bitten by the Vampire Squirrel...

She bared her
new fangs in a
broad vampire
smile, and gave
the fake princess
the biggest shock
of his life. He

dropped the emperor and fled.

Ping-Pong landed head-first in a bowl of bird's nest soup laid out on the banqueting table.

Hurrying into action, the Kung-Fu Pigs took up their fighting positions…

The stage was
set for a battle…

Get them!

The Crimson Trotter sent his wolfish
henchmen into the fray.

Rinki and Stinki fought as never before.

It was too much for the wolves...

And cursing the Kung-Fu Pigs for spoiling his evil plans, the Crimson Trotter crept out into the night.

CHAPTER 9

"Are not victory and defeat but two sides of the same coin?"
Ti-Fu, 1st century fool

The Kung-Fu Pigs were victorious. The Crimson Trotter's plans lay in ruins, and his gang of wolves took to their paws and fled. Of the Crimson Trotter himself, not a trace remained.

The emperor, young Ping-Pong, had by now come round from his own terrible ordeal. He was shaken, but saved.

"What h-happened? Didn't she want to marry me?"

The others looked to Dinki to explain.

"No, your Highness, that wasn't the real princess. It was one of the Crimson Trotter's wicked wolves. He planned to kidnap you and steal your throne."

"The fiend!" sniffed Ping-Pong.

Rinki learnt from a captured bandit that the real Princess Yukkifoto had been imprisoned at another fortress high in the hills. They would have to find her and bring her to the temple. Her worried father, I-Shu-Koko, said he would head there at once.

And then we must prepare for another wedding!

But the emperor wasn't sure he could face another wedding ceremony just yet, and went off to take a bath and catch up on some sleep.

And what of Manki Hanki? Dinki discovered her wandering in the darkened cellar and led her back to the emperor's litter while they pondered her future.

Now the great temple was deserted but for the Kung-Fu Pigs and a mountain of wedding banquet. Stinki licked his lips.

"Why don't we finish off this lot? There'll be no wedding today and there's no point in wasting good food!"

Rinki nodded and sat down in front of a large roast carp. "Later we should take the vampire Manki Hanki back to Oinky No Ho. Perhaps he'll be able to rid her of the Curse of the Vampire Squirrels."

"I agree," answered noble Dinki. "She did save the emperor's life, after all."

And so the Kung-Fu Pigs enjoyed a huge wedding banquet, the emperor Ping-Pong slept in his beautiful room, and the Crimson Trotter contemplated the fact that his latest plan lay in ruins!

Enjoy your triumph while you can, meddlesome pigs! I will return with a new and better plan!
Not for a while, I hope!

EPILOGUE

So it was, that the Kung-Fu Pigs rescued the emperor once again. Later that week, Ping-Pong finally married Princess Yukkifoto and peace returned once again to our kingdom.

Manki Hanki, that most loyal of royal nannies, was freed of her curse, thanks to the powerful prayers of the holy temple and a stiff exercise regime, though she may never be able to look a squirrel in the eye again.

The Kung-Fu Pigs returned to their everyday lives, but were ready as ever to answer the emperor's call whenever it should come.

But now I hear the bell tolling and I must

go to prayer. Depart in peace, and walk the path of truth, honourable stranger…

THE END